Sonia's Extra-Special Dish

by Fernando Rodney
illustrated by Karo

Harcourt
SCHOOL PUBLISHERS

Printed in China

ISBN 10: 0-15-350512-5
ISBN 13: 978-0-15-350512-6

Ordering Options
ISBN 10: 0-15-350334-3 (Grade 4 Below-Level Collection)
ISBN 13: 978-0-15-350334-4 (Grade 4 Below-Level Collection)
ISBN 10: 0-15-357501-8 (package of 5)
ISBN 13: 978-0-15-357501-3 (package of 5)

2 3 4 5 6 7 8 9 10 985 12 11 10 09 08 07

Characters

Narrator	Mr. Garces	Ms. Florence	Sonia
Andre	Mom	Sara	Dad
Nicole	Grandmama	Andy	

Setting: Meadow Grammar School

Narrator: The afternoon sun sparkles through the window as Mr. Garces explains fractions to his fourth-grade class. Suddenly, a visitor arrives. It's Ms. Florence, the principal here at Meadow Grammar School.

Ms. Florence: Hello, everyone. I have exciting news today.

Andre: We're getting out early?

Ms. Florence: No, Andre. However, I'm absolutely certain you'll like this. On the fifteenth, our school is having an International Day.

Sara: What's that?

Ms. Florence: It's a fair that will show what we've learned about world culture. We'll have an extensive array of activities for everyone's parents and friends. There will be plays, music, dancing, art, and games. Each class will have a particular job.

Nicole: What will we do?

Ms. Florence: I'm recruiting you for a very special task. I'd like the fourth graders to bring the food.

Andy: Oh, so we have the most important job.

Ms. Florence: Many would agree. Mr. Garces told me that you've been talking about cultural heritage in social studies. We thought you could each bring a dish that reflects your family's heritage.

Sonia: How do we do that?

Mr. Garces: Bring something from your family's native country, or maybe a dish that you serve on a holiday.

Narrator: The bell rings.

Mr. Garces: All right, everyone. Start thinking about what you'll bring!

Narrator: Sonia walks pensively up the driveway, her eyes downcast. She is in such deep thought that she almost walks into her father at the mailbox.

Dad: Hey, there!

Sonia: Oh, I'm sorry, Dad! I was busy thinking about something I have to do for school.

Dad: Maybe I can help. What is it?

Sonia: We're having an International Day. Everyone in the fourth grade has to bring in food that reflects our heritage. I don't know what to bring.

Dad: Well, your grandmother taught me lots of dishes that she learned while growing up in Poland.

Sonia: That's great! What should we make?

Dad: How about my favorite—*pierogi*?

Sonia: What are they?

Dad: I've made them for you before. They're the little dumplings made out of dough. You fill them with potatoes and cheese, or meat. Then you boil them. Then you fry them. They're delicious!

Sonia: Oh, I know what you mean! That's perfect! Will you help me?

Dad: Of course I will!

Narrator: Sonia runs into the house. Her mother is in the living room, working at her computer.

Sonia: Hi, Mom!

Mom: Hi, Sonia! How was school?

Sonia: It was fine. On the fifteenth, we're having an International Day. You and Dad are invited.

Mom: That sounds fun. Do you have to do anything?

Sonia: I have to bring a dish that's part of my culture.

Mom: You're in luck! Think of all the wonderful Indian food that your grandmother makes. She's a culinary genius. We could make one of her dishes.

Sonia: I—

Mom: We'll cook together! It will be reminiscent of my childhood. Some of my most vivid memories are of your Grandmama at the stove, serenely making the most wonderful smelling food. Her cooking was legendary in our family. Let's see . . . why don't we make a curry?

Sonia: Which one is curry?

Mom: Curry is a mixture of spices that are pounded into a paste. Then you add that to meat, fish, or vegetables. All the different spices taste fantastic! Let's make that. All right?

Sonia: All right.

Narrator: Sonia flops on her bed and mutters to herself.

Sonia: What am I going to do? Dad thinks I'm going to make something Polish to reflect his heritage. Mom expects me to make something Indian because of her heritage. How do I choose one over the other? I don't want to deprive anyone!

Narrator: Sonia's cat, Star, jumps on the bed and stares solemnly at her. Sonia strokes the cat's silky hair.

Sonia: Oh, Star, what am I going to do?

Narrator: Sonia's Grandmama has come to dinner.

Mom: We're going to need your help, Mama. Sonia is going to make a curry to bring to her school's International Day.

Dad: I thought Sonia was going to make my mother's *pierogi*.

Narrator: Both Mom and Dad look at Sonia with some consternation. Sonia averts her eyes. A queasy feeling rises in her stomach.

Sonia: I'm sorry. I know you both want me to make something from your culture. How can I choose?

Grandmama: You don't have to choose.

Narrator: Sonia gapes at Grandmama, stunned at her words.

Grandmama: I have an idea . . .

Narrator: International Day has commenced. The fourth graders bring out their dishes.

Mr. Garces: Everything looks wonderful! What's that, Sara?

Sara: I brought *dim sum*, Japanese steamed dumplings.

Andy: I have my mom's *arroz con pollo*—the best chicken and rice in the world!

Nicole: I have *Nanaimo* bars. They're a Canadian dessert. There's a cookie bottom, then a layer of vanilla pudding, and chocolate on top.

Andre: Mmm! I'm moving to Canada!

Ms. Florence: Sonia, that smells terrific. What is it?

Sonia: I made *pierogi*. They're Polish dumplings.

Mr. Garces: Oh, so your dish is Polish.

Sonia: Sort of—*pierogi* are usually filled with potatoes and cheese, or meat. We filled ours with curried chicken. Curry is a mix of Indian spices that you pound into a paste. Then you cook meat, fish, or vegetables with the curry.

Ms. Florence: Then your dish is Indian, too?

Sonia: Exactly. My father is Polish, and my mother is Indian. I love both their cultures, so I didn't want to choose one over the other. Then my Grandmama had the idea—I'm a mix of both cultures. Why not mix both foods?

Mr. Garces: That's a great idea!

Narrator: Andy tastes one of Sonia's curried *pierogi*.

Andy: It tastes great, too!

Sonia: See? Both parts of my heritage are special on their own, but when you mix them together, you get something extra special!

Think Critically

1. Why does Sonia have to choose a food to bring to school?
2. How is Sonia's dish different from the others in her class?
3. Why doesn't Sonia tell her mother that she already has an idea for a dish from her father?
4. How would you describe Sonia?
5. Do you think it's important to learn about your cultural heritage? Why or why not?

Art

Comic Strip Choose a section of this story. Retell it in comic strip form, using pictures and dialogue balloons.

School-Home Connection Talk with a family member about different foods that are important to your family or your culture.

Word Count: 1,003

Science Sight Word Readers™

Heart

by Justin McCory Martin

ISBN 978-0-545-24799-3

Photographs © 2010: cover: Corbis Images/India Picture; back cover top: iStockphoto/Suprijono Suharjoto; back cover bottom: iStockphoto/Sebastian Kaulitzki; page 1: iStockphoto/Nina Shannon; page 2: Masterfile; page 3: iStockphoto/Mads Abildgaard; page 4: iStockphoto/John Woodcock; page 5 top: iStockphoto/Yunus Arakon; page 5 bottom: iStockphoto/Jason Lugo; page 6: ShutterStock, Inc./Fenton; page 7: iStockphoto/Roman Dekan; page 8: ShutterStock, Inc./Attl Tibor; page 9: ShutterStock, Inc./Rob Marmion; page 10: Getty Images/Tim Ridley; page 11: Getty Images/John Giustina; page 12: iStockphoto/Suprijono Suharjoto; page 13 left: iStockphoto/Tatiana Gladskikh; page 13 top right: ShutterStock, Inc./decu; page 13 center top right: iStockphoto/Benjamin Brandt; page 13 center right: iStockphoto/Klaudia Steiner; page 13 center bottom right: ShutterStock, Inc./Alex Staroseltsev; page 13 bottom right: iStockphoto/Michael Krinke; page 14: iStockphoto/Elena Elisseeva; page 15: iStockphoto/Roman Dekan; page 16: iStockphoto/Mads Abildgaard.

Photo research by Veroniqua Quinteros; Design by Holly Grundon

12 11 10 9 8 7 6 5 4 3 2   10 11 12 13 14 15/0

Printed in the U.S.A.   40

First printing, September 2010

SCHOLASTIC INC.

NEW YORK • TORONTO • LONDON • AUCKLAND
SYDNEY • MEXICO CITY • NEW DELHI • HONG KONG

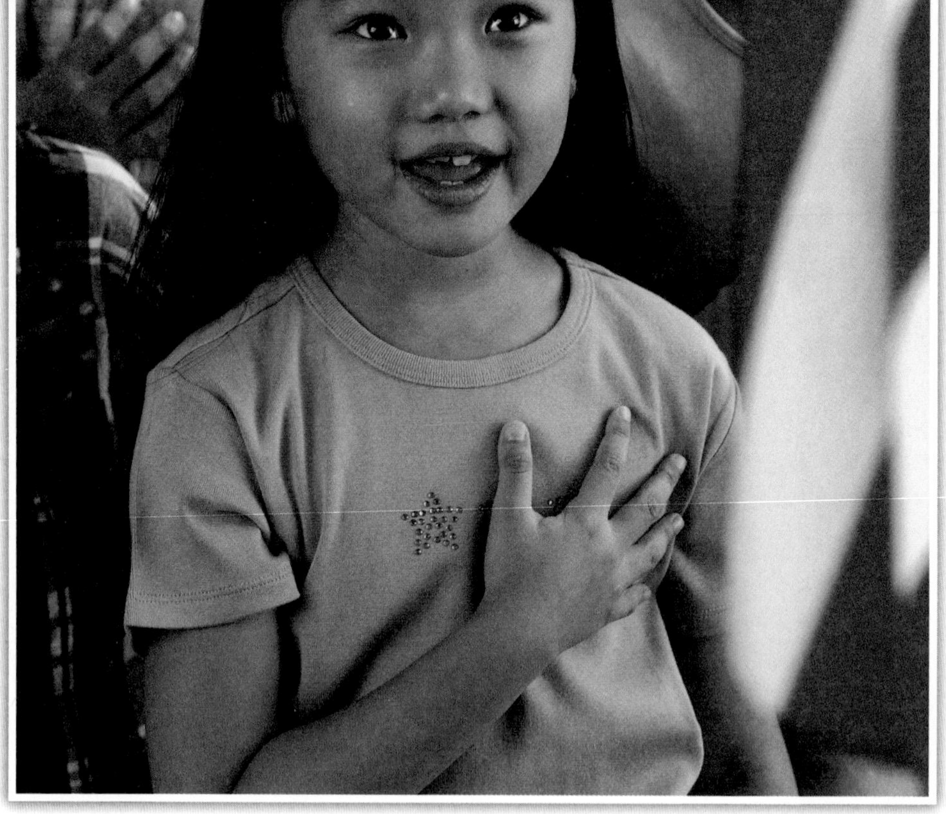

Your **heart beats**.

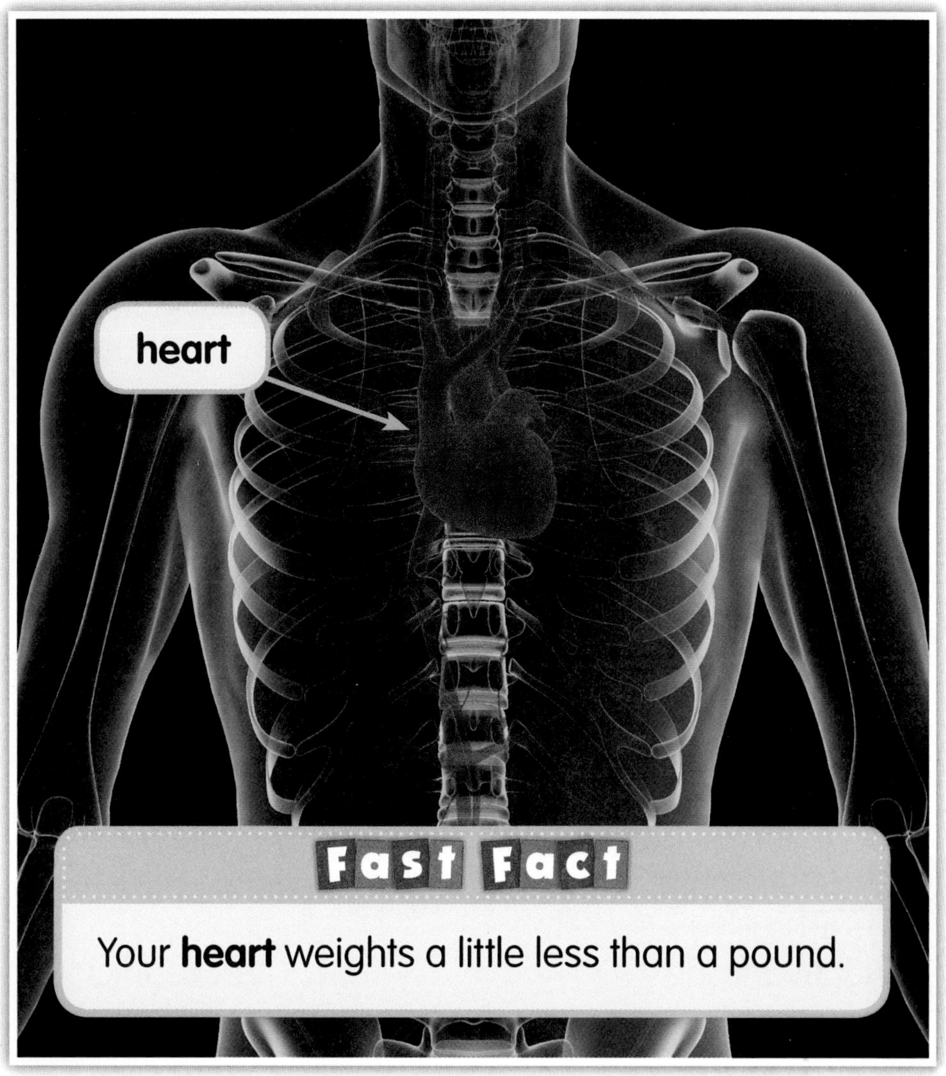

Fast Fact

Your **heart** weights a little less than a pound.

It **beats** inside your chest.

Heart Parts

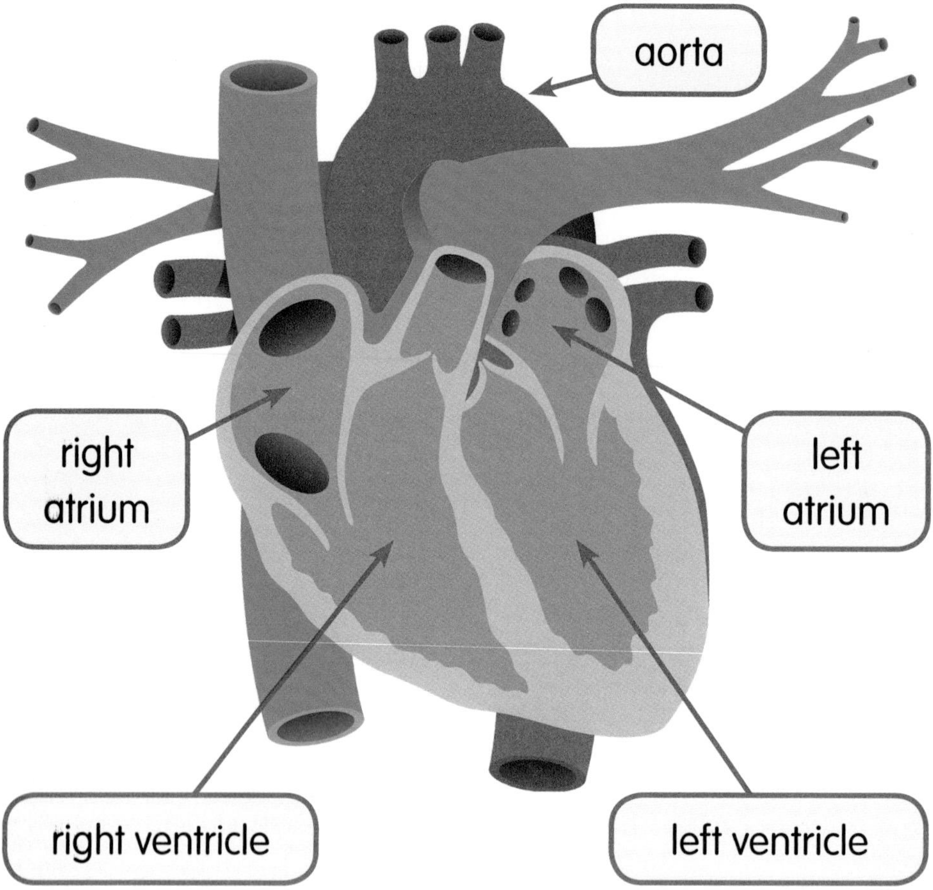

Your **heart beats**.

It has many parts.

Fast Fact

A kid's **heart** is about the size of a fist.

Your **heart beats**.

It is a super-strong muscle.

Take A Look

This is what **blood** looks like under a microscope.

Your **heart beats**.

It pumps **blood**.

Circulatory System

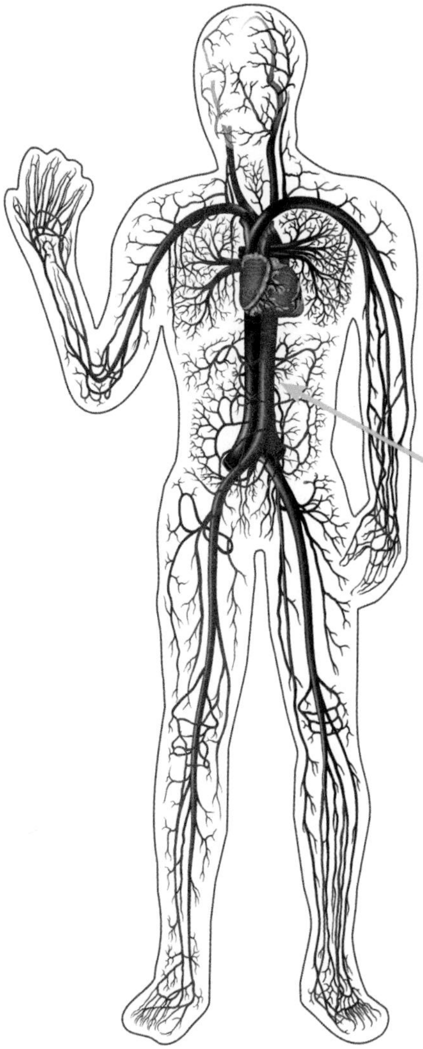

Fast Fact

It takes about one minute for **blood** to travel from your **heart** through your **whole** body.

Your **heart beats**. It sends **blood** to your **whole** body.

Fast Fact

Your **heart beats** about 2 ½ billion times during your life.

Your **heart beats**. It keeps going your **whole** life.

Fast Fact

Your **heart beats** faster when you exercise.

Your **heart beats**. It goes a **whole** lot faster when you run.

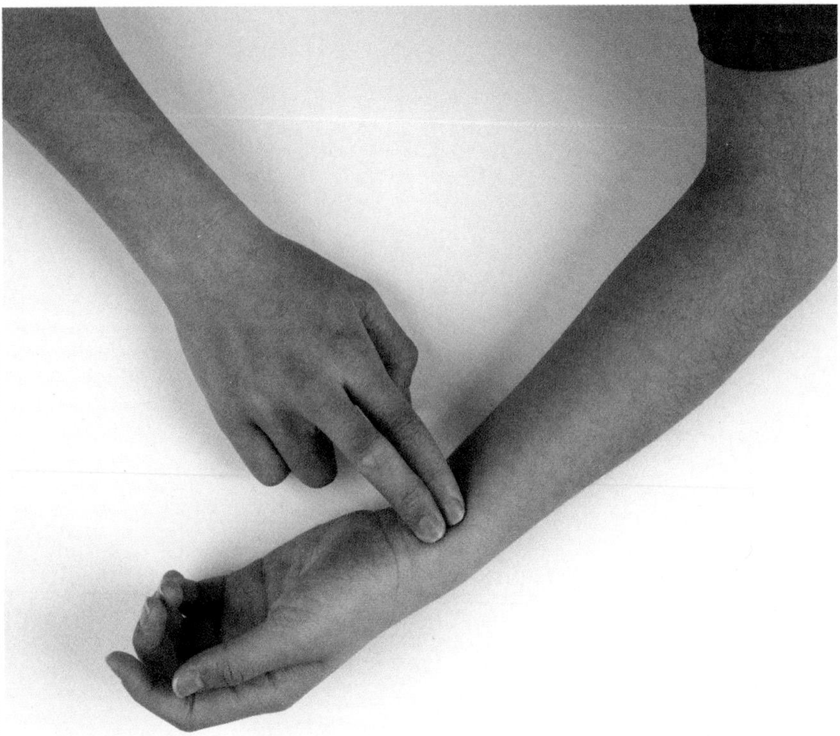

Try This!

Touch your wrist. Can you feel the pulse? This is caused by your **heart** pumping.

Your **heart beats**.

You can feel it.

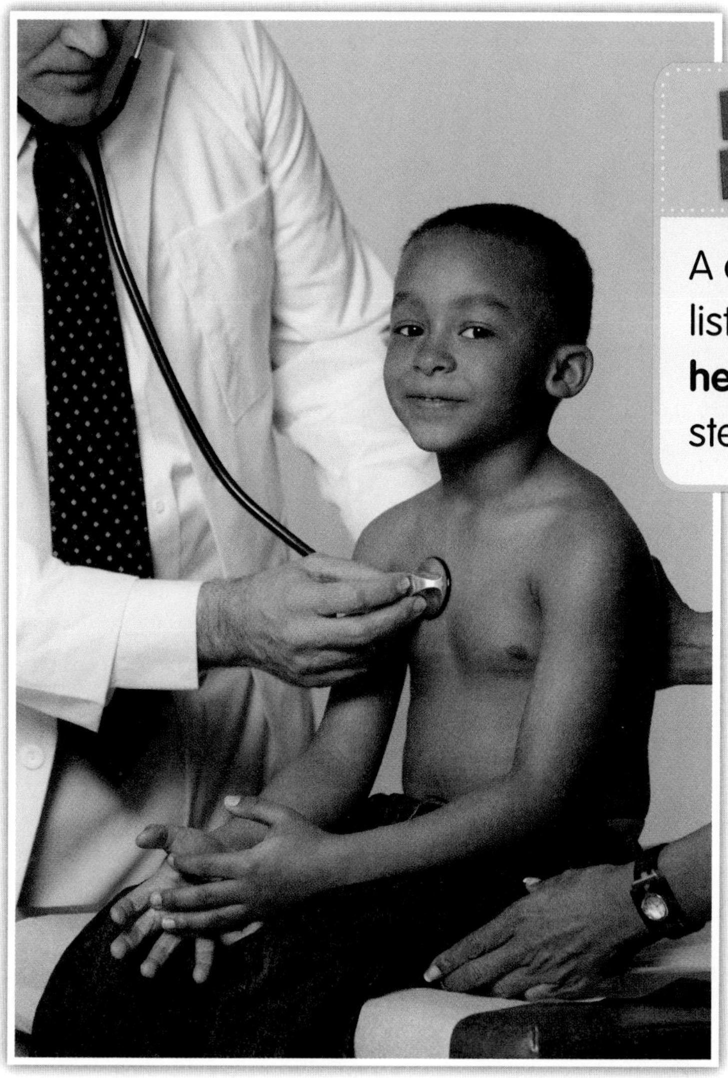

Fast Fact

A doctor can listen to your **heart** with a stethoscope.

Your **heart beats**.
You can hear it.

Fast Fact

Exercise helps keep your **heart** strong.

Your **heart beats**.

Take good care of it...

Fast Fact

These foods are good for your **heart**.

vegetables

bread

fruit

fish

chicken

...and the **beat** will go on and on.

Sight Word Review

Point to each sight word. Then read it aloud.

Sight Word Fill-ins

Use one sight word from the box to finish each sentence.

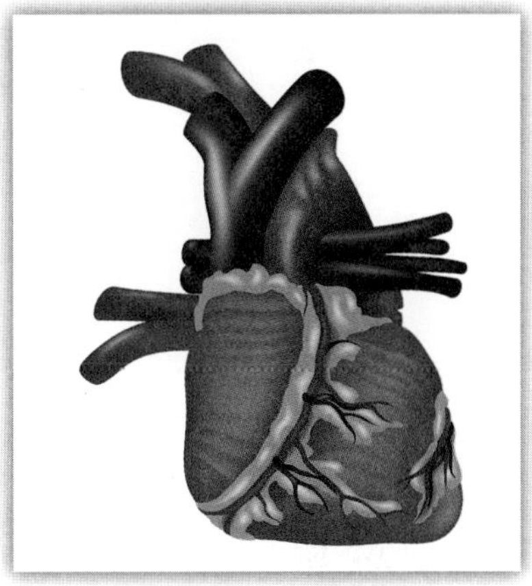

beats	**blood**
heart	**whole**

1. Your ______ is inside of your chest.
2. Your heart ______ about 2 ½ billion times in your life!
3. Your heart pumps ______.
4. Your heart beats for your ______ life.

ANSWERS: 1. heart 2. beats 3. blood 4. whole

All About Your Heart

Ask a grown-up to read this with you.

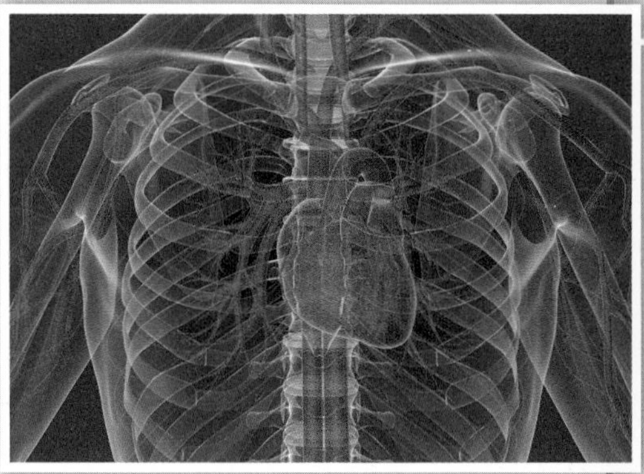

Your heart is a muscle. It's about the size of your fist. It's located in the middle of your chest, just a little to the left.

Your heart is like a pump. With each beat, your heart fills with blood. Then it squeezes the blood out into your body. Blood travels through tubes called blood vessels. Blood carries oxygen to every part of your body: your brain, your stomach, even the tips of your toes. You could not survive without your heart's hard work.

Lub-dub, lub-dub. That's the sound of a heartbeat. A doctor can hear that sound through a stethoscope. A baby's heart beats 130 times a minute. As you grow older, your heartbeat slows down. An adult's heart beats between 60 and 100 times each minute. That's a whole lot of heartbeats—2½ billion in your lifetime. Take care of your heart by exercising and eating healthy foods such as fish and fresh fruit.